Do you ever wish there were magic answers to all your problems? Do you want to know if you'll ever get a puppy or a kitten? Do you wonder how to deal with your annoying little sister? Do you want to find out if you'll do well in your exams? Well, this special book has ALL the answers. Mind you, I wouldn't always trust Tracy Beaker and her friends to know absolutely everything!

This is a fun way to solve all your little niggling queries. Think of a question, open the book anywhere you like, and see what the advice is on the right-hand page. If you don't like the answer, you can always try all over again.

You can keep a record of your questions on the left-hand page, and write about your daily life, confiding all your secret thoughts. Many of my favourite fictional characters keep journals. This is your chance to write about your life in this special book.

I kept a journal right throughout my childhood. I'd often ask myself questions too. They were often very silly, like *Could I grow long blond hair down to my waist?* When I was a teenager I frequently asked my diary *How will I ever get a proper boyfriend?* But the question I asked over and over again was this one: *Will I get to be a writer when I grow up?* Most of my journal dreams have come true. I hope yours do too!

Jacquelin

DATE

Jacqueline Wilson

Illustrated by
NICK SHARRATT

☆☆☆ ASK ☆☆☆ TRACY BEAKER ☆☆ and Friends ☆☆

CORGI

☆ Tracy says ☆
I DARE YOU TO!

DATE

☆ Beauty says ☆

YOU'LL FEEL BETTER IF YOU CUDDLE YOUR PET

DATE

☆ Hetty says ☆

IT'S TIME TO GO ON A JOURNEY

☆ Mr Speed says ☆

TAKE UP
A NEW SPORT

DATE

☆ India says ☆

KEEPING A DIARY HELPS YOU SORT OUT YOUR THOUGHTS

DATE

☆ Sadie says ☆

JUST LET IT ALL OUT!

DATE

☆ Violet says ☆

DO SOMETHING CREATIVE

DATE

☆ Ruby says ☆

IT WON'T BE AS EMBARRASSING AS YOU THINK

DATE

☆ Charlie says ☆

TRY MEETING
YOUR NEIGHBOURS

DATE

☆ Miranda says ☆

YOU'LL BE BOWLED OVER!

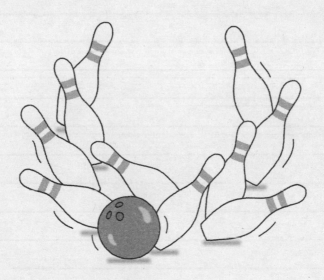

DATE

☆ Tracy says ☆

JUST GO FOR A BURGER!

DATE

⭐ Gemma says ⭐

YOU CAN RELY ON A REALLY GOOD FRIEND

DATE

☆ Em says ☆

CHOOSE A GOOD ROLE MODEL

DATE

DON'T LET YOURSELF BE BOSSED AROUND

⭐ Prue says ⭐

THERE'S MORE TO LIFE THAN MAKE-UP

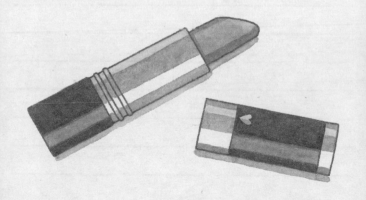

☆ Tracy says ☆

IT'S TIME TO RELAX

DATE

☆ Mandy says ☆

BE KIND
TO SOMEONE
YOU LOVE

☆ Claire says ☆

TRY NOT TO WORRY

DATE

☆ Sylvie says ☆

BE CAREFUL

☆ Beauty says ☆

DON'T GIVE UP

DATE

☆ Tracy says ☆

DON'T BE SCARED

DATE

☆ Treasure says ☆

NO!

DATE

☆ Ruby and Garnet say ☆

STICK TOGETHER

☆ Hetty says ☆

BE BRAVE

DATE

☆ Daisy says ☆

REMEMBER WHO YOUR REAL FRIENDS ARE

DATE

☆ Lizzie says ☆

DO SOMETHING FUN

DATE

DATE

☆ Sadie says ☆

MAKE SOMEONE LAUGH

DATE

☆ Lottie says ☆

WORK HARD

DATE

☆ Em says ☆

MAKE THE MOST OF IT

DATE

☆ Elsa says ☆

CHEER EVERYONE UP WITH A JOKE

☆ Cam says ☆

ENJOY SIMPLE PLEASURES

DATE

☆ Gemma says ☆

APPRECIATE
YOUR FAMILY

DATE

☆ Prue says ☆

FOLLOW
YOUR HEART

DATE

☆ Floss says ☆

SHARE YOUR FAVOURITE STORY

☆ Ellie says ☆

LOVE THE WAY YOU LOOK

DATE

DATE

☆ Beauty says ☆
USE YOUR TALENTS

DATE

☆ Sadie says ☆

TAKE IT IN
YOUR STRIDE

☆ Dolphin says ☆

TRY TO REMEMBER THE GOOD TIMES

DATE

☆ Tracy says ☆

COME UP WITH
A NEW IDEA

☆ Hetty says ☆

HOLD FAST TO
YOUR DREAMS

DATE

☆ Lizzie says ☆

SMILE!

DATE

☆ Mandy says ☆

HONESTY IS THE BEST POLICY

☆ Daisy says ☆

STICK UP FOR WHAT YOU KNOW IS RIGHT

☆ Tracy says ☆

BE A STAR!

DATE

☆ Charlie says ☆

TALK TO SOMEONE YOU TRUST

DATE

☆ Sylvie says ☆

PHONE A FRIEND

☆ Ruby says ☆

AIM HIGH

☆ Rax says ☆

SET THE WORLD ALIGHT!

DATE

☆ Tracy says ☆

MIX UP SOME MAGIC

DATE

☆ Gemma says ☆

MAKE YOUR FEELINGS KNOWN

DATE

☆ Pearl says ☆

MAKE A WISH

DATE

☆ Dixie says ☆

MUCK IN
AND HELP

DATE

☆ Sadie says ☆

THINK ABOUT YOUR FUTURE

DATE
_____
_____
_____
_____
_____
_____
_____
_____
_____
_____
_____
_____
_____
_____
_____
_____
_____
_____
_____
_____
_____
_____
_____

☆ Tracy says ☆

I DARE YOU
NOT TO!

DATE

☆ Andy says ☆

LOOK FOR FRIENDS
IN UNEXPECTED
PLACES

☆ Ruby says ☆

INTREPID EXPLORERS USE NATURAL RESOURCES!

☆ Gemma and Alice say ☆

ENJOY A
GOOD MEAL

☆ Tracy says ☆

HAVE A LAUGH!

⭐ Elsa says ⭐

BE AS TOUGH AS OLD BOOTS

DATE

☆ Lizzie says ☆
LEND A HAND

DATE

☆ Em says ☆

SHARE THE FUN

DATE

☆ Lottie says ☆

MAKE THE
MOST OF NEW
EXPERIENCES

☆ Ellie says ☆

EMBARRASSING MOMENTS DON'T LAST FOR EVER

DATE

☆ Cam says ☆

WRAP UP WARM

DATE

☆ Tanya says ☆

KEEP IN TOUCH WITH OLD FRIENDS

DATE

☆ Tim says ☆

HANG ON
IN THERE!

DATE
_____
_____
_____
_____
_____
_____
_____
_____
_____
_____
_____
_____
_____
_____
_____
_____
_____
_____
_____
_____
_____
_____

☆ Jade says ☆

GO FOR A RUN TO RELAX

DATE
_____
_____
_____
_____
_____
_____
_____
_____
_____
_____
_____
_____
_____
_____
_____
_____
_____
_____
_____
_____
_____
_____

☆ Football says ☆

KEEP WORKING
ON YOUR SKILLS

DATE

☆ Holly says ☆

LET SOMEONE ELSE TAKE CARE OF YOU SOMETIMES

☆ Treasure says ☆

TAKE COMFORT IN
A GOOD BOOK

TURN TO SOMEONE YOU CAN TRUST

DATE

☆ Ellie says ☆

LOOKS AREN'T
EVERYTHING

DATE

☆ Tracy says ☆

SOMETIMES YOU CAN HAVE YOUR CAKE AND EAT IT!

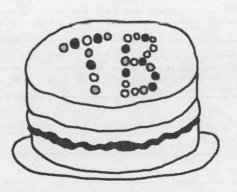

DATE

⭐ Biscuits says ⭐

BE YOUR OWN
SUPERHERO!

☆ Beauty says ☆

YOU'RE NEVER TOO OLD FOR YOUR TEDDY

DATE
_____

☆ Daisy says ☆

DON'T BE TAKEN IN BY APPEARANCES

DATE

☆ India says ☆

REAL FRIENDS
ARE THE BEST

DATE

☆ Verity says ☆

KNOW WHEN
TO SAY GOODBYE

DATE

☆ Tracy says ☆

STAND UP FOR YOURSELF

DATE

☆ Tanya says ☆

REMEMBER HOW LUCKY YOU ARE

⭐ Elsa says ⭐

IT'S NOT ALWAYS THE RIGHT TIME FOR A JOKE

DATE

☆ Lizzie says ☆

GIVE NEW PEOPLE A CHANCE

☆ Cam says ☆

YOU DESERVE
A TREAT

DATE
_____
_____
_____
_____
_____
_____
_____
_____
_____
_____
_____
_____
_____
_____
_____
_____
_____
_____
_____
_____
_____
_____

☆ Gemma says ☆

GET STUCK IN!

DATE

☆ Lola Rose says ☆

FACE YOUR FEARS

DATE

☆ Sadie says ☆

US GIRLS STICK TOGETHER

☆ Charlie says ☆
SURPRISE YOURSELF!

☆ Tracy says ☆

HIT THE JACKPOT!

☆ William says ☆

EVERYBODY IS GOOD AT SOMETHING

☆ Biscuits says ☆

ALWAYS TAKE
SUPPLIES!

☆ Ruby says ☆

GET YOUR
OWN BACK!

DATE

☆ Floss says ☆

BE PROUD
OF YOURSELF

DATE

☆ Tracy says ☆

USE YOUR
IMAGINATION

DATE
_____
_____
_____
_____
_____
_____
_____
_____
_____
_____
_____
_____
_____
_____
_____
_____
_____
_____
_____
_____
_____

☆ Gemma says ☆

TRY DOING
SOMETHING NEW

☆ Ruby says ☆

JUST BE YOURSELF

DATE

☆ Elsa says ☆

YOU CAN BE
A STAR

DATE

☆ Tracy says ☆

YOU KNOW WHO
YOU CAN TRUST

Who'll look after Elsie
when she's left all alone?

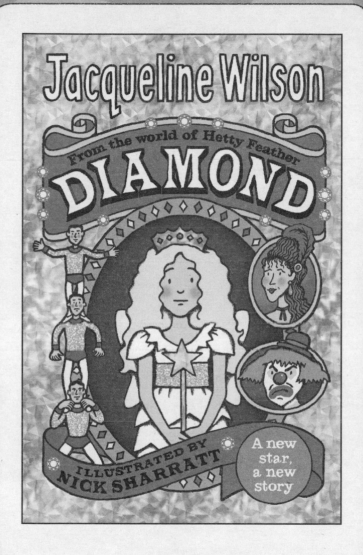

Jacqueline Wilson

From the world of Hetty Feather

DIAMOND

ILLUSTRATED BY
NICK SHARRATT

A new
star,
a new
story

From the world of
Hetty Feather

CHECK OUT JACQUELINE WILSON'S OFFICIAL WEBSITE!

There's lots of fun stuff including games, amazing competitions and exclusive news. You can even customise your own page and start your own online diary!

Find out all about Jacqueline in her monthly diary and blog, read her fan-mail replies, and chat to other fans on the message boards.

Join in today at
www.jacquelinewilson.co.uk

And to view the exciting book trailers including *The Worst Thing About My Sister*, *Queenie* and *Diamond*, visit Jacqueline's official YouTube channel at **www.youtube.com/ JacquelineWilsonTV**

ASK TRACY BEAKER AND FRIENDS
A CORGI BOOK 978 0 552 56998 9

First published in Great Britain by Doubleday,
an imprint of Random House Children's Publishers UK
A Random House Group Company

Hardback edition published 2010
This edition published 2014

1 3 5 7 9 10 8 6 4 2

Compiled by Alexandra Antscherl

The Random House Group Limited supports the Forest Stewardship
Council® (FSC®), the leading international forest-certification organisation.
Our books carrying the FSC label are printed on FSC®-certified paper.
FSC is the only forest-certification scheme supported by the leading
environmental organisations, including Greenpeace. Our paper procurement
policy can be found at www.randomhouse.co.uk/environment.

MIX
Paper from
responsible sources
FSC® C016897

Set in Blueprint MT

Random House Children's Publishers UK,
61–63 Uxbridge Road, London W5 5SA

www.randomhousechildrens.co.uk
www.totallyrandombooks.co.uk
www.randomhouse.co.uk

Addresses for companies within The Random House Group Limited
can be found at: www.randomhouse.co.uk/offices.htm

THE RANDOM HOUSE GROUP Limited Reg. No. 954009

A CIP catalogue record for this book is available from the British Library.

Printed and bound in Great Britain by CPI Group (UK) Ltd, Croydon CR0 4YY